O9-ABF-276

George and Martha

The Complete Stories of Two Best Friends

GEORGE AND MARTHA

AND

THE COMPLETE STORIES OF TWO BEST FRIENDS

JAMES MARSHALL

With an introduction by Maurice Sendak

Houghton Mifflin Company Boston 1997

Introduction copyright © 1997 by Maurice Sendak

GEORGE AND MARTHA • Copyright © 1972 by James Marshall

GEORGE AND MARTHA ENCORE • Copyright © 1973 by James Marshall

GEORGE AND MARTHA RISE AND SHINE • Copyright © 1976 by James Marshall

GEORGE AND MARTHA ONE FINE DAY • Copyright © 1978 by James Marshall

GEORGE AND MARTHA TONS OF FUN • Copyright © 1980 by James Marshall

GEORGE AND MARTHA BACK IN TOWN • Copyright © 1984 by James Marshall

GEORGE AND MARTHA ROUND AND ROUND • Copyright © 1988 by James Marshall

Afterword copyright © 1995 by Houghton Mifflin Company

Library of Congress Cataloging-in-Publication Data
Marshall, James, 1942–1992
George and Martha: the complete stories of two best friends / by James Marshall.
p. cm.
Contents: George and Martha — George and Martha encore — George and Martha
rise and shine — George and Martha one fine day — George and Martha
tons of fun — George and Martha back in town — George and Martha round and round.
ISBN 0-395-85158-0
1. Children's stories, American.
[1. Hippopotamus — Fiction. 2. Friendship — Fiction. 3. Short stories.] I. Title.
PZ7.M45672Gcf 1997
[E] — dc21 96-47572 CIP AC

Manufactured in the United States of America
DOC 10 9 8 7 6 5 4 3 2 1

Dedications

GEORGE AND MARTHA
For George and Cecille

GEORGE AND MARTHA ENCORE
For Adolph, Adrienne, Ronald, and Philip

GEORGE AND MARTHA RISE AND SHINE
For my father

GEORGE AND MARTHA ONE FINE DAY
For my nephew
Alexander Christian Schwartz

GEORGE AND MARTHA TONS OF FUN
For Maurice Sendak

GEORGE AND MARTHA BACK IN TOWN
For Rhoda Dyjak

GEORGE AND MARTHA ROUND AND ROUND
For my mother

  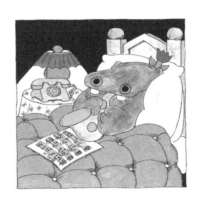

CONTENTS

FOREWORD 1

GEORGE AND MARTHA 7

GEORGE AND MARTHA ENCORE 53

GEORGE AND MARTHA RISE AND SHINE 101

GEORGE AND MARTHA ONE FINE DAY 147

GEORGE AND MARTHA TONS OF FUN 195

GEORGE AND MARTHA BACK IN TOWN 243

GEORGE AND MARTHA ROUND AND ROUND 291

AFTERWORD 339

FOREWORD

The picture book is a peculiar art form that thrives on genius, intuition, daring, and a meticulous attention to its history and its various, complex components. The picture book is a picture puzzle, badly misunderstood by critics and condescended to by far too many as merely a trifle for "the kiddies." Children are routinely patronized, and thus so are we who spend our creative lives entertaining them and nourishing their spirit. Given this minefield of confusions and uncertainties, when such a work turns out looking as easy as a James Marshall picture book, it says everything about the man. Marshall is the last of a long line of masters that began in the late nineteenth century with the preeminent English illustrator, Randolph Caldecott; then continued in our century with Jean de Brunhoff in France and Edward Ardizzone in England; and then via Tomi Ungerer arrived full blast in America, where the laurel wreath settled finally, splendidly, on the judicious, humane, witty, and astonishingly clever head of James Marshall.

James paid close attention to the history of his craft; he loved "the business" and brought to it all the many gifts bestowed on him—his passion for music and literature, his sly comic timing, a delicate sense of restraint and order, and that eerie instinct for just the right touch and tone. Perhaps best of all, his work was enriched by his enormous capacity for friendship. That was another gift. James the perfect friend was indistinguishable from James the perfect artist. The voice, the pulse, the heart of his words and pictures were always pure, authentic Marshall. You got the whole man.

If I remember with terrible pain my lost friend and colleague, it is only because James raised the art of friendship to an exhilarating height. I think myself the luckiest of men to have shared his sweet warmth and confidence. There is a small army of people who, I'm certain, feel the same way. He made me laugh until I cried. No one else could ever do that. He was a wicked angel and will be missed forever.

James scolded, gossiped, bitterly reproached, but always loved and forgave. All these qualities were generously funneled into his work, and there is no better example than the George and Martha books to showcase the dazzling kaleidoscope of Marshalliana. The inspiration for these two tender hippos goes back to James' shrewd appraisal of those books that most stimulated his impatient, creative intellect. He relished the extraordinary wit and brevity of the French children's books of the 1930s and the solemn, mock-serious tone of the English books of the same period. He borrowed and swiped—we all do, we all must—and it was riveting to watch James stalk, attack, and drain away the riotous madness from a favorite Tomi Ungerer and skillfully, hilariously, Marshall it.

With his first George and Martha book, James was already entirely himself. He lacked only one component in his constellation of gifts: he was uncommercial to a fault. No shticking, no nudging knowingly, no winking or pandering to the grown-ups at the expense of the kids. He paid the price of being maddeningly underestimated—of being dubbed "zany" (an adjective that drove him to murderous rage). And worse, as I saw it, he was dismissed as the artist who *could* do—*should* or *might* do—worthier work if he would only dig deeper and harder. The comic note, the delicate riff were deemed, finally, insufficient. James knew better, of course, and he was right, of course, but he suffered nevertheless. There was nothing he could do to impress the establishment; that was his triumph and his curse. Marshall *did* fulfill his genius, and its rarity and subtlety confounded the so-called critical world. The award givers were foolish enough to consider him a charming lightweight, and when Caldecott Medal time came around, they ignored him again and again.

What James couldn't know was that history was playing a nasty trick on him; "the business" was changing, seemingly overnight. The dear old cottage industry and its healthy idealism, the co-mingling of writer, artist, editor, production director, designer, printer, and binder, the thrumming collaboration that my generation took for granted—all gone in this new, media-bedeviled, marketing-mad Business, which has no interest in history or time for fine-grooming the fires of talent, which mindlessly shoots gifted youngsters out of the big-bucks cannon and ruthlessly lets them fall where they may. The apprenticing so critical for the development of new writers and illustrators is a thing of the past. Where, I wonder, do the new kids go, now that the old solid ground rules are corrupted and not to be trusted. It must all begin again. But history waits to be remembered, and if Marshall is, as I claim, the last of the line, then he is, too, the beginning of the next time around.

Marshall's work is undated, fresh and fragrant as a new spring garden. Nothing says this better than this twenty-fifth anniversary edition of all thirty-five George and Martha stories. If one of James' most remarkable attributes was his genius for friendship, then George and Martha are the quintessential expression of that genius. Those dear, ditzy, down-to-earth hippos bring serious pleasure to everybody, not only to children. They are time-capsule hippos who will always remind us of a paradise in publishing and—both seriously and comically—of the true, durable meaning of friendship under the best and worst conditions.

The George and Martha books teach us nothing and everything. That is Marshall's way. Just when you are lulled by the ease of it all, he pokes you sharply. My favorite poke comes at the end of "The Surprise" in *George and Martha Round and Round*. When George has "a wicked idea" and hoses Martha down "one late summer morning," Martha screams "Egads!" and declares war on George. Nothing he can say will soothe her wrath, but Martha suffers the consequences of her inability to forgive. She can't tell George a funny story she's read or tell him a joke she's heard because "she and George were no longer on speaking terms." But a falling autumn leaf does the trick. It's George's favorite season, so Martha goes straight to her old friend's house and they make up and watch the autumntime together. "Good friends just can't stay cross for long," George comments. "You can say that again," says Martha. A neat, sweet ending? Not a chance. Turn the page and there is a demented-looking Martha (how *did* Marshall convey dementia, malice, and get-evenness with two mere flicks of his pen for eyes?), spritzing hose in hand, lying in wait for dapper George with fedora and cane to cross her path. Marshall's last line: "But when summer rolled around again, Martha was ready and waiting."

Much has been written concerning the sheer deliciousness of Marshall's simple, elegant style. The simplicity is deceiving; there is richness of design and mastery of composition on every page. Not surprising, since James was a notorious perfectionist and endlessly redrew those "simple" pictures. The refined sensibilities of his hippos stand in touching contrast to their obvious tonnage, and his pen line—though never forgetting their impossible weight and size—endows them with the grace and airiness of a ballerina and her cavalier. The great white splash at the end of "The High Board" in *George and Martha Back in Town* is a marvel of weight on white, with a squiggly line to delineate the shuddering catastrophe of a diving hippopotamus. Marshall says dryly: "Martha caused quite a splash."

I admit to favoring Martha; she never forgets and rarely forgives altogether, and she gets the best Marshall lines. "The Diary" from *George and Martha One Fine Day* has her toughest, yummiest exit line. In fact, that particular book showcases Martha, and we see her there at her glorious, unstable best.

Detailing the George and Martha stories, though irresistible, is certainly unnecessary. Old fans will renew acquaintance in this volume, but it is the new fans I am counting on. The hippos are charming—that's plain. The surprise will come to the young artists amidst those young fans when they discover the exquisite artistry, the architecture, behind the "easy" look of it all; the quiet dignity of Marshall's work, the astonishing integration of style and form, the hint of history; the animal gestures that betray their passionate sources, opera and ballet and vaudeville and TV and movies, cartoons, paintings, travel; the gamut, simply, of the fertile genius of James Marshall.

As I write this on a lovely spring afternoon and glimpse out the window the miracle of my old weeping cherry tree cascading pink blossoms, after having spent many happy hours studying and recollecting and missing James, I am reminded of a line, now full of new meaning, from "The Last Story" in *George and Martha Encore*. Out of love for Martha, and to ease her misery over her messy garden, George stuffs store-bought tulips into the ground. Martha catches him, and George is embarrassed. But Martha is moved. "Dear George," she says. "I would much rather have a friend like you than all the gardens in the world."

MAURICE SENDAK

May 1997

4

GEORGE AND MARTHA

THE COMPLETE STORIES OF TWO BEST FRIENDS

Five
Stories About
Two Great
Friends

Story
Number
One

Split Pea Soup

Martha was very fond of making split pea soup. Sometimes she made it all day long. Pots and pots of split pea soup.

If there was one thing that George was *not* fond of, it was split pea soup. As a matter of fact, George hated split pea soup more than anything else in the world. But it was so hard to tell Martha.

One day after George had eaten ten bowls of Martha's soup, he said

to himself, "I just can't stand another bowl. Not even another spoonful."

So, while Martha was out in the kitchen, George carefully poured

the rest of his soup into his loafers under the table. "Now she will think

I have eaten it."

But Martha was watching from the kitchen.

"How do you expect to walk home with your loafers full of split pea soup?" she asked George.

"Oh dear," said George. "You saw me."

"And why didn't you tell me that you hate my split pea soup?"

"I didn't want to hurt your feelings," said George.

"That's silly," said Martha. "Friends should always tell each other the truth. As a matter of fact, I don't like split pea soup very much myself. I only like to make it. From now on, you'll never have to eat that awful soup again."

"What a relief!" George sighed.

"Would you like some chocolate chip cookies instead?" asked Martha.

"Oh, that would be lovely," said George.

"Then you shall have them," said his friend.

STORY NUMBER TWO

The Flying Machine

"I'm going to be the first of my species to fly!" said George.

"Then why aren't you flying?" asked Martha. "It seems to me that you are still on the ground."

"You are right," said George. "I don't seem to be going anywhere at all."

"Maybe the basket is too heavy," said Martha.

"Yes," said George, "I think you
are right again. Maybe if I climb out, the
basket will be lighter."

"Oh dear!" cried George. "Now what have I done? There goes my flying machine!"

"That's all right," said Martha. "I would rather have you down here with me."

The Tub

STORY NUMBER THREE

George was fond of peeking in windows.

One day George peeked in on Martha.

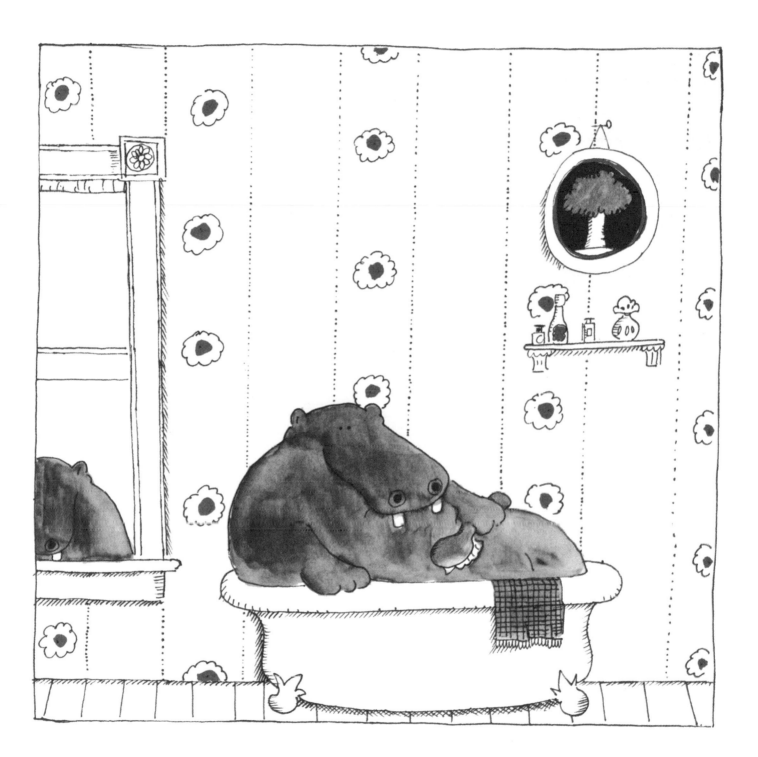

He never did *that* again.

"We are friends," said Martha. "But there is such a thing as privacy!"

STORY NUMBER FOUR

The Mirror

"How I love to look at myself in the mirror," said Martha.

Every chance she got, Martha looked at herself in the mirror.

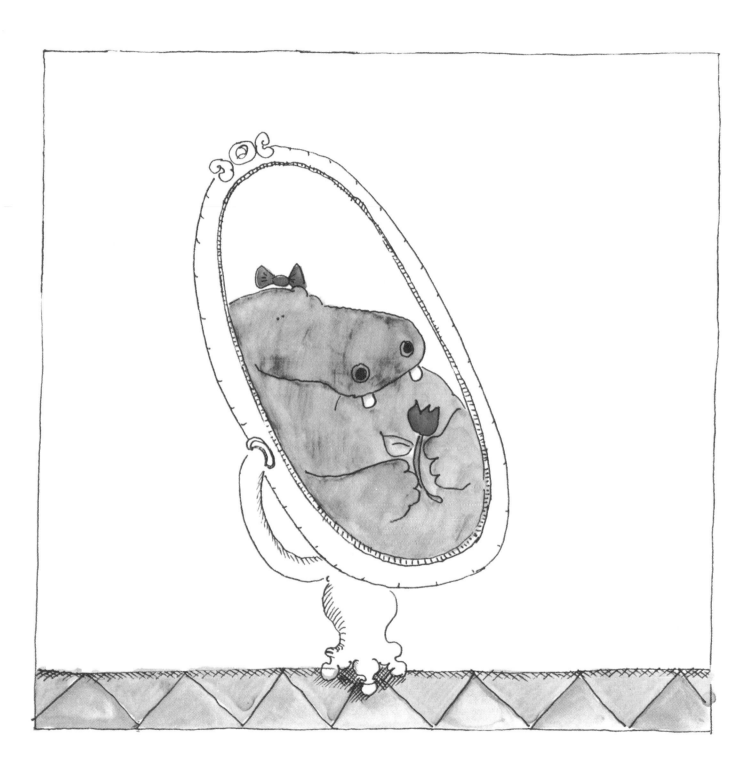

Sometimes Martha even woke up during the night to look at herself.

"This is fun." She giggled.

But George was getting tired of watching Martha look at herself in the mirror.

One day George pasted a silly picture he had drawn of Martha onto the mirror.

What a scare it gave Martha. "Oh dear!" she cried. "What has happened to me?"

"That's what happens when you look at yourself too much in the mirror," said George.

"Then I won't do it ever again," said Martha.

And she didn't.

THE LAST STORY

The Tooth

One day when George was skating to Martha's house, he tripped and fell. And he broke off his right front tooth. His favorite tooth too.

When he got to Martha's, George cried his eyes out.

"Oh dear me!" he cried. "I look so funny without my favorite tooth!"

"There, there," said Martha.

The next day George went to the dentist.

The dentist replaced George's missing tooth with a lovely gold one.

When Martha saw George's lovely new golden tooth, she was very happy. "George!" she exclaimed. "You look so handsome and distinguished with your new tooth!"

And George was happy too. "That's what friends are for," he said. "They always look on the bright side and they always know how to cheer you up."

"But they also tell you the truth," said Martha with a smile.

MORE STORIES ABOUT TWO GREAT CHUMS

~

STORY NUMBER ONE

THE DANCE RECITAL

George and Martha were having a disagreement.

"I think dancing is dumb," said George.

"Dancing is not dumb!" exclaimed Martha.

"Dancing is fun! And if you don't come to my dance recital, I'll be very angry!"

So, of course, George went to Martha's recital.

"I'm going to hate this," he said to himself.

But what a surprise for George!

Martha's Dance of the Happy Butterfly

was so impressive.

"Dancing looks like fun," said George.

The next day George went to dancing class.

"You see," said Martha, "dancing is fun!"

Very soon George was in his own dance recital.
Martha said that his Mexican Hat Dance was
the best she had ever seen.

THE SECOND STORY

THE FRENCH LESSON

George went to Martha's house for his French lesson.

"Bonjour, Martha," said George.

"Bonjour, George," said Martha.

George sat next to Martha on the sofa.

"How do you say 'Give me a kiss' in French?" asked George.

"You say 'Voulez-vous m'embrasser?'"* answered Martha.

*(This sounds like "Voo-lay-voo mom-brass-ay?")

And that is just what George did.

"Tee-hee," said Martha.

"I knew you were going to do that."

STORY NUMBER THREE

THREE

THE DISGUISE

George decided to dress up as an Indian.

"This disguise will really fool Martha," he chuckled.

"She'll never recognize me."

But Martha wasn't fooled a bit.

"Hi, George," she said.

"Why are you wearing that Indian costume?"

George was so disappointed.

He walked away hanging his head.

Martha felt simply awful.

She hadn't meant to hurt George's feelings.

"George," said Martha. "I would never have recognized you if it hadn't been for your bright smiling eyes. It's so hard to disguise smiling eyes."

And, of course, George felt much, much better.

STORY NUMBER FOUR

THE BEACH

One day George and Martha went to the beach.

"I love the beach!" exclaimed Martha.

"So do I," said George.

"However, we must be sure to put on our suntan lotion."

But Martha refused to put on her suntan lotion.

"You'll be sorry," George called out.

"Oh, pooh," said his friend.

"You're a fuss-budget, George."

Martha was having such a lovely time.

The next day Martha had a terrible sunburn!

She felt all hot and itchy.

But George never said "I told you so."

Because that's not what friends are for.

THE LAST STORY

STORY

THE GARDEN

Martha was so discouraged.

Her garden was an ugly mess of weeds.

"I just don't seem to have a green thumb," she sobbed.

George hated to see Martha unhappy.

He wanted so much to help.

Suddenly George had a splendid idea.

He went to the florist and bought

all the tulips in the shop.

Tulips were Martha's favorite flowers.

Very quietly George crept into Martha's garden

and stuck the tulips in the ground.

But just then Martha happened to look out the window.

"Oh, dear," said George.

"You're always catching me."

But Martha was so pleased.

"Dear George," she said.

"I would much rather have a friend like you

than all the gardens in the world."

FIVE STORIES

ABOUT
TWO FINE FRIENDS

STORY NUMBER ONE
THE FIBBER

One day George wanted to impress Martha.

"I used to be a champion jumper," he said.

Martha raised an eyebrow.

"And," said George, "I used to be a wicked pirate."

"Hmmm," said Martha.

George tried harder. "Once I was even
a famous snake charmer!"

"Oh, goody," said Martha.

Martha went to the closet and got out Sam.

"Here's a snake for you to charm."

"Eeeek," cried George.

And he jumped right out of his chair.

"It's only a toy *stuffed* snake," said Martha. "I'm
   surprised a famous snake charmer is such a scaredy-cat."

"I told some fibs," said George.

"For shame," said Martha.

"But you can see what a good jumper I am," said George.

"That's true," said Martha.

Martha was in her laboratory.

"What are you doing?" asked George.

"I'm studying fleas," said Martha.

"Cute little critters," said George.

"You don't understand," said Martha.

"This is serious. This is science."

The next day, George noticed that Martha was scratching a lot. She looked uncomfortable.

George bought Martha some special soap. After her shower Martha felt much better.

"I think I'll stop studying fleas," said Martha.

"Good idea," said George.

"I think I'll study bees instead," said Martha.

"Oh dear," said George.

STORY NUMBER 3

THE PICNIC

One Saturday morning, George wanted to sleep late.

"I love sleeping late," said George.

But Martha had other ideas.

She wanted to go on a picnic.

"Here she comes!" said George to himself.

Martha did her best to get George out of bed.

"Picnic time!" sang Martha.

But George didn't budge.

Martha played a tune on her saxophone.

George put little balls of cotton in his ears and pulled up the covers.

Martha tickled George's toes.

"Stop it!" said George.

"Picnic time!" sang Martha.

"But I'm *not* going on a picnic!" said George.

"Oh yes you *are*!" said his friend.

Martha had a clever idea.

"This is such hard work," she said, huffing and puffing.

"But I'm not going to help," said George.

"I'm getting tired," said Martha.

George had fun on the picnic.

"I'm so glad we came," said George.

But Martha wasn't listening.

She had fallen asleep.

Martha was nervous.

"I've never been to a scary movie before."

"Silly goose," said George. "*Everyone* likes scary movies."

"I hope I don't faint," said Martha.

Martha *liked* the scary movie. "This is fun," she giggled.

Martha noticed that George was hiding under his seat.

"I'm looking for my glasses," said George.

"You don't wear glasses," said Martha.

When the movie was over, George was as white as a sheet.

"Hold my hand," George said to Martha. "I don't want
 you to be afraid walking home."

"Thank you," said Martha.

THE LAST STORY

THE SECRET CLUB

"Where are you going, George?" asked Martha.

"I'm going to my secret club," said George.

"I'll come along," said Martha.

"Oh no," said George, "it's a secret club."

"But you can let *me* in," said Martha.

"No I can't," said George. And he went on his way.

Martha was furious.

When George was inside his secret clubhouse, Martha made a terrible fuss.

"You let me in," she shouted.

"No," said George.

"Yes, yes," cried Martha.

"No, no," said George.

"I'm coming in whether you like it or *not*!" cried Martha.

When Martha saw the inside of George's clubhouse, she was so ashamed.

"You old sweetheart," she said to George.

George smiled. "I hope you've learned your lesson."

"I certainly have," said his friend.

One morning when George looked out his window,
he could scarcely believe his eyes. Martha
was walking a tightrope.
"My stars!" cried George. "I could *never* do that!"
"Why not?" said Martha. "It's tons of fun."

"But it's so high up," said George.

"Yes," said Martha.

"And it's such a long way down," said George.

"That's very true," said Martha.

"It would be quite a fall," said George.

"I see what you mean," said Martha.

Suddenly Martha felt uncomfortable.

For some reason she had lost all her confidence.

She began to wobble.

George realized his mistake.

Now he had to do some fast talking.

"Of course," he said, "anyone can see you love walking the tightrope."

"Oh, yes?" said Martha.

"Certainly," said George. "And if you love what you do, you'll be very good at it too."

Martha's confidence was restored.

"Watch this!" she said. Martha did some fancy footwork on her tightrope.

STORY NUMBER TWO

THE DIARY

Whenever Martha sat down to write in her
diary, George was always nearby.

"Yes, George?" said Martha.

"I was just on my way to the kitchen," said George.

"Hum," said Martha.

Martha decided to finish writing outdoors.

"How peculiar," she said to herself. "I can

still smell George's cologne."

Then Martha heard leaves rustling above her.

"Aha!" she cried. "You were spying on me!"

"I wanted to see what you were writing in your diary," said George.

"Then you should have asked my permission," said Martha.

"May I peek in your diary?" asked George politely.

"No," said Martha.

At lunch George started to tell an icky story.

Martha strongly objected.

"Please, have some consideration," she said.

But George told his icky story nevertheless.

"You're asking for it," said Martha.

When Martha finished her lunch, *she* told
an icky story. It was so icky that George
felt all queasy inside. He couldn't even
eat his dessert.

"You're the champ," said George.

"Don't make me do it again," said Martha.

"I won't," said George.

STORY NUMBER FOUR

THE BIG SCARE

"Boo!" cried George.

"Have mercy!" screamed Martha.

Martha and her stamp collection went flying.

"I'm sorry," said George. "I was feeling wicked."

"Well," said Martha. "Now it's my turn."

"Go ahead," said George.

"Not right away," said Martha slyly.

Suddenly George found it very difficult to concentrate on what he was doing.

"Any minute now, Martha is going to scare the pants off me," he said to himself.

"Maybe she is hiding someplace," he said.
George made sure that Martha wasn't hiding
under the sink.

During the day George
got more and more nervous.
"Any minute now," he said.

But Martha was relaxing in her hammock.

"I'm sorry I forgot to scare you," said Martha.

"That's all right," said George. "It wouldn't have worked anyway. I'm not easily frightened."

"I know," said Martha.

THE LAST STORY

THE AMUSEMENT PARK

That evening George and Martha
went to the amusement park.
They rode the ferris wheel.

They rode the roller coaster.

They rode the bump cars.

They were having a wonderful time.

But in the Tunnel of Love, Martha

sat very quiet.

It was very very dark in there.

Suddenly Martha cried "Boo!"

"Have mercy!" screamed George.

"I didn't forget after all," said Martha.

"So I see," said George.

.

FIVE STORIES ABOUT THE BEST OF FRIENDS

STORY NUMBER ONE

THE MISUNDERSTANDING

George was practicing his handstands.

"This calls for concentration," he said.

Suddenly the doorbell rang.

It was Martha.

"I've come to chat," she said.

"Not this afternoon," said George.

"I want to be alone."

"I hope Martha understands," said George.

But Martha did not understand.

Martha was offended.

Martha was hurt.

And Martha was *mad!*

A few minutes later, George's telephone rang.

It was Martha.

"George," she said, "I never want to see you again!"

And she slammed down the receiver.

"Oh dear," said George.

Martha was mad all afternoon and evening.

Finally she got out her saxophone.

"This will calm me down," she said.

Soon Martha was having quite a bit of fun.

In fact she was having *so* much fun that she
didn't even answer her telephone.

"Oh dear," said George. "Martha must still
be upset."

But Martha had forgotten all about the
misunderstanding.

STORY NUMBER TWO

THE SWEET TOOTH

George had a sweet tooth.

He just couldn't stop himself from eating sweets.

"You know what they say about too much sugar,"
said Martha.

"Let's not discuss it," said George.

Late at night George would raid the refrigerator
to satisfy his sweet tooth.

"You'll weigh a ton," said Martha.

"Let's not discuss it," said George.

"This calls for action!" said Martha.

And she lighted up a cigar.

"Stop that!" cried George. "You'll make yourself sick!"

"Let's not discuss it," said Martha.

"You'll ruin your teeth!" cried George.

"We won't discuss it," said Martha.

"Please!!" cried George. "You're ruining your health."

"No discussion," said Martha.

Martha began to turn a peculiar color.

George couldn't stand it any longer,

and he fell to his knees.

"I'll do anything you say!" he begged.

"Will you cut down on your sweets?"

said Martha.

"I promise," said George.

And Martha put out her cigar.

STORY NUMBER THREE

THE PHOTOGRAPH

One day Martha stepped into a
photography booth.
"I love to have my picture taken,"
she said.
"Click," went the camera.

When Martha saw her photograph,
she was thrilled.
"I've never looked prettier," she said.

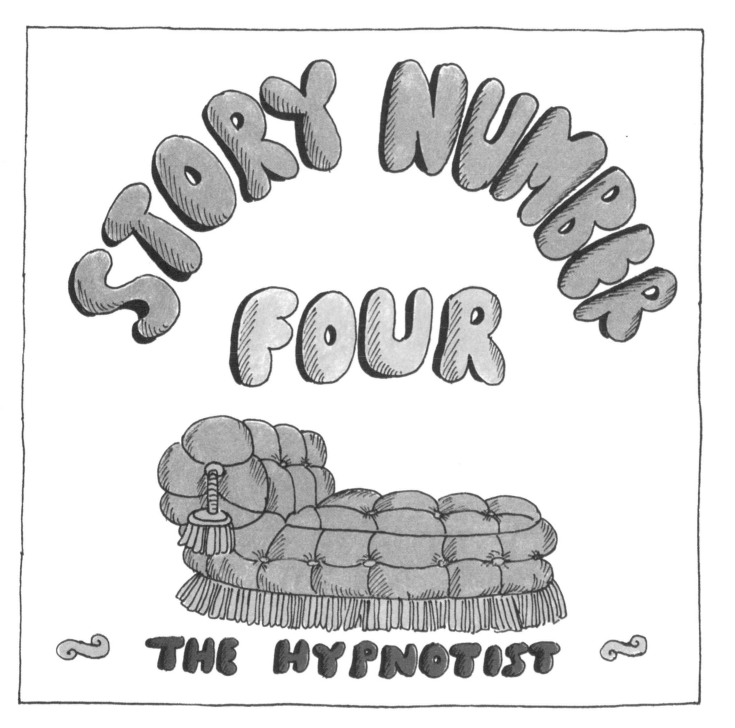

George was trying to hypnotize Martha.

"Your eyes are getting heavy," said George.

"I believe they are," said Martha.

"You are getting sleepy," said George.

"That's true," said Martha.

And in a moment Martha seemed sound asleep.

"Success!" whispered George.

Ever so quietly George tiptoed to the kitchen,
where he kept his cookie jar.

"Ah-ha!" cried Martha.

George was ashamed.

He'd broken his promise.

"Would you like a cookie?" he asked Martha.

"Yes, I would!" she said.

And she ate them all.

THE LAST STORY

THE SPECIAL GIFT

It was George's birthday, and Martha
stopped by the bookshop to buy a gift.
"He loves to read," Martha told the
salesperson.

On the way to George's house,
Martha played a tricky game of
hopscotch.

George could hardly wait for his gift.

"I can't stand the suspense," he said.

But when Martha went to look for George's

book, it wasn't there.

"I'm waiting," said George.

"What will I do?" said Martha to herself.

"I'm waiting," said George.

Martha quickly decided to give George
the photograph of herself.
"It's not much," she said.
When George saw Martha's picture,
he fell off his chair laughing.
"*Well!*" said Martha. "What's so funny?"

"This is the best gift I've ever received,"
  said George.

"It *is*?" said Martha.

"Of course," said George. "It's wonderful to have
  a friend who knows how to make you laugh."
  Martha decided to swallow her pride.
  She saw that the photograph was pretty funny
  after all.

Five Stories

About

Two Dear Friends

*

Story Number One

THE BOX

Martha noticed a little box
on George's kitchen table.
"Do not open," said the sign.
"I won't," said Martha.
"I'm not the nosy type."
But Martha couldn't take her eyes off
the little box.
She read the sign again.
"Do not open," said the sign.
Martha couldn't stand it.
"One little peek won't hurt," she said.
And she untied the string.

Out jumped George's entire collection of
Mexican jumping beans.

"Oh my stars," said Martha.

It took Martha all afternoon
to round up the Mexican jumping beans.
One yellow one gave her quite a chase.

When George came home

Martha was reading a magazine.

"You seem out of breath," said George.

"You don't think I opened that little box,

do you?" said Martha.

"Of course not," said George.

"I'm not the nosy type," said Martha.

George didn't say a word.

STORY NUMBER TWO
THE HIGH BOARD

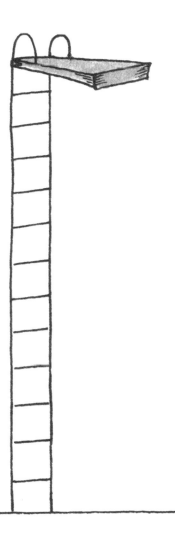

"Today," said George, "I will jump from
  the high board!"

"Don't do it!" cried Martha.

"Everyone will be watching!" said George.

"You'd never catch *me* up there!" said Martha.

"That's because you're a scaredy-cat," said George.

But when George got up on the high board,

he lost his nerve.

"I can't do it," he said.

"And everyone is watching!"

His knees began to shake.

"I'll be right up," said Martha.

Martha climbed up the ladder.

"Now what?" said George.

"I'll go first," said Martha.

And she jumped off.

Martha caused quite a splash.

Everyone was impressed.

And no one noticed how George got down.

"I just didn't feel like it today," said George.

Martha didn't say a word.

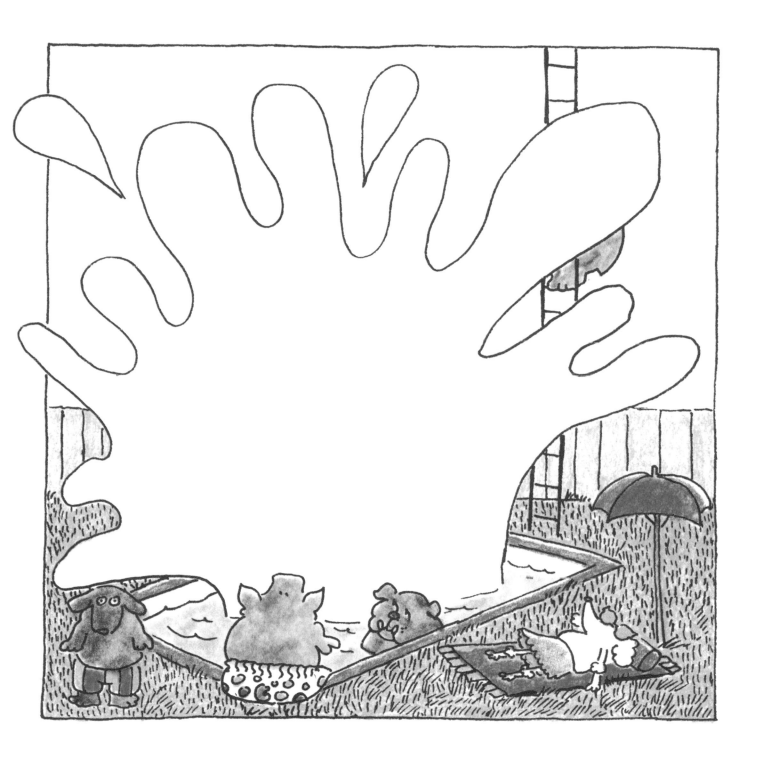

STORY NUMBER
THREE

THE TRICK

George was fond of playing tricks on Martha.

But that was not Martha's idea of fun.

And when she found her house slippers

nailed to the floor, she was not amused.

Martha gave George the old

silent treatment.

"Oh no!" said George. "Not that!"

George decided to bake Martha's favorite cake.

"This will butter her up," he said.

When the cake was done,

George put it in a box.

And he went to look for a pretty ribbon.

"I have a surprise for you," said George.

"It's another trick!" said Martha.

"Not this time," said George.

"Then *you* open it," said Martha.

"Very well," said George. "I will."

Martha bit her nails, while George
pulled off the ribbon.

Out jumped one rubber tarantula,

one stuffed snake, four plastic spiders,

and two real frogs!

"Egads!" cried George. "I've been tricked!"

"And by the way," said Martha.

"The cake was simply delicious."

STORY NUMBER FOUR

THE JOB

George was excited about his new job.

"It's hard work," said Martha.

"You must be *very* strict."

"I'll try," said George.

"No horsing around is allowed!"
said Martha.

"Thanks for the advice," said George.

"That's what friends are for,"
said Martha.

Very soon George saw that someone
was disobeying the rules.

"No horsing around!" he called through
his megaphone.

"It's all right!" shouted Martha.

"It's only me!"

"You heard me!" called out George.

George meant business.

And he gave Martha quite a bawling out.

"Well!" said Martha,

"And I thought we were friends!"

"Oh dear," said George. "Martha was right —
this *is* a hard job!"

George was all nice and cozy.

"May I join you?" said Martha.

"I'm reading," said George.

"I'll be as quiet as a mouse," said Martha.

"Thank you," said George.

And he went back to his book.

But soon Martha was fidgeting.

"Please!" said George.

"Have some consideration!"

"Sorry," said Martha.

George went back to his reading.

But in no time Martha was fidgeting again.

"That does it!" said George.

And he left.

At home he got all nice and cozy again.

He opened his book.

"It is important to be considerate
to our friends," said the book.

"It certainly *is!*" said George.

"Sometimes we are thoughtless without even
knowing it," said the book.

"*I'll* say!" said George.

"Martha should read this book."

He went to find her.

"I'm sorry I was fidgeting," said Martha.

"I got lonely."

"Oh," said George. "I never considered that."

"What did you want to tell me?" said Martha.

"Oh nothing," said George.

"I just got lonely too."

And they sat and told stories into the night.

Martha didn't fidget even once.

FIVE STORIES ABOUT THE BEST OF FRIENDS

STORY NUMBER ONE

THE CLOCK

George gave Martha a present
for her birthday.

"It's a cuckoo clock," said George.

"So I see," said Martha.

"It's nice and loud," said George.

"So I hear," said Martha.

"Do you like it?" asked George.

The next day

George went to Martha's house.

Martha was not at home.

And the cuckoo clock

was not on the wall.

"Maybe she likes it so much

she took it with her," said George.

Just then he heard a faint

"Cuckoo . . . cuckoo . . . cuckoo."

To George's surprise,

the cuckoo clock was at the bottom

of Martha's laundry basket.

When Martha returned,
she couldn't look George in the eye.
"It must have fallen in by mistake,"
she said. "I do hope it isn't broken."
"Not at all," said George.
"The paint isn't even chipped,
the clock works just dandy,
and the cuckoo hasn't lost
its splendid voice."

"Would you like to borrow it?"

asked Martha.

George was delighted.

He found just the right spot for it, too.

Wasn't that considerate of

Martha to lend me her clock? thought George.

"Cuckoo," said the clock.

STORY NUMBER TWO

THE TRIP

George invited Martha

on an ocean cruise.

"Is *this* the boat?" said Martha.

"Use your imagination," said George.

"I'll try," said Martha.

Very soon it was raining cats and dogs.

"This is unpleasant," said Martha.

"Use your imagination," said George.

"Think of it as a thrilling storm

at sea."

"I'll try," said Martha.

"Lunch is served," said George.

And he gave Martha a soggy cracker.

Martha was not impressed.

"Use your imagination," said George.

"Oh looky," said Martha.

"What a pretty shark."

"A shark!" cried George.

George took a spill.

"But where's the shark?" he said.

"Really," said Martha.

"You must learn to use
  your imagination."

STORY NUMBER

THREE

THE ARTIST

George was painting in oils.

"That ocean doesn't look right," said Martha.

"Add some more blue.

And that sand looks all wrong.

Add a bit more yellow."

"Please," said George.

"Artists don't like interference."

But Martha just couldn't help herself.

"Those palm trees look funny," she said.

"That does it!" said George.

"See if you can do better!"

And he went off in a huff.

"My, my," said Martha.

"Some artists are *so* touchy."

And she began to make

a few little improvements.

When George returned

Martha proudly displayed the painting.

George was flabbergasted.

"You've ruined it!" he cried.

"I'm sorry you feel that way," said Martha.

"I like it."

Martha was one of those artists

who aren't a bit touchy.

STORY NUMBER FOUR

THE ATTIC

One cold and stormy night
George decided to peek into the attic.

"Go on up," said Martha.

"Oooh no," said George.

"There might be a ghost up there,
or a skeleton, or a vampire,
or maybe even some werewolves."

"Oooh goody!" said Martha.

"Let's investigate!"

But there wasn't much to see in the attic,

only a box of old rubber bands.

George was disappointed.

"Would you like to hear a story

that will give you goose bumps?" asked Martha.

"You bet," said George.

"When you hear it, your bones will go cold,"

said Martha.

"Oooh," said George.

"Your blood will curdle," said Martha.

"Ooooh," said George.

"And you'll feel mummy fingers

up and down your spine," said Martha.

"Stop!" cried George. "I can't take any more.

Tell me some other time!"

That night Martha went to bed
with the light on.
She had a bad case of goose bumps.

One late summer morning
George had a wicked idea.
"I shouldn't," he said.
"I really shouldn't."
But he just couldn't help himself.
"Here comes the rain!" he cried.
"Egads!" screamed Martha.

Martha was thoroughly drenched
and as mad as a wet hen.
"That did it!" she said.
"We are no longer on speaking terms!"
"I was only horsing around,"
said George.
But Martha was unmoved.

The next morning, Martha read a funny story.

"I can't wait to tell George," she said.

Then she remembered that she and George
were no longer on speaking terms.

Around noon Martha heard a joke on the radio.

"George will love this one," she said.

But she and George weren't speaking.

In the afternoon Martha observed
the first autumn leaf fall to the ground.

"Autumn is George's favorite season," she said.

Another leaf came swirling down.

"That does it," said Martha.

Martha went straight to George's house.

"I forgive you," she said.

George was delighted to be back
on speaking terms.

"Good friends just can't stay cross
for long," said George.

"You can say that again,"
said Martha.

And together they watched the
autumn arrive.

But when summer rolled around again,
Martha was ready and waiting.

AFTERWORD

Born in San Antonio, Texas, in 1942, James Marshall never planned to become a children's book author and illustrator. He attended the New England Conservatory of Music and played the viola. But a physical accident ended his career, and he then studied French and history, receiving a master's degree at Trinity College.

For a time Marshall supported himself by teaching French and Spanish in a Boston school. Although he would eventually teach students at Parsons School of Design in New York City, he was an untrained artist. Meanwhile he doodled, placing eyes and lines to create characters. Eventually those doodles reached an editor, who gave Marshall his first illustrating assignment, *Plink, Plink, Plink* (1971) by Byrd Baylor. His next book, which came out the following year, was to demonstrate to adults and children the potential that Marshall possessed: *George and Martha*, a collection of five vignettes about two hippopotamuses who have a unique friendship, was enthusiastically received by children. As Marshall was later to say, he knew with this book that he had found his life's work. That life's work was to last for twenty years and bring about the creation of dozens of picture books and novels, including six more George and Martha books, Harry Allard's *Miss Nelson Is Missing!* (1977), Ogden Nash's *Adventures of Isabel* (1991), *The Stupids Die* (1981), *Fox and His Friends* (1982), and *The Cut-Ups* (1984).

Marshall's talent was wide-ranging; he had an intuitive grasp of how to reduce a visual object to its most basic elements, the type of genius found in the sculptures of Alexander Calder. Marshall's most famous characters, George and Martha, were created with two dots for eyes, a nose, and a mouth. Marshall's compositions depend on his line rather than his color; he began publishing books when artists were still required to create color separations, and even in his later books he always retained his strong black line.

From Marshall's notebooks, available among other places at the De Grummond Collection at Hattiesburg, Mississippi, it is immediately apparent that he drew with great spontaneity and energy. But unlike many artists who lose this spontaneity in the books themselves, Marshall kept it in abundance. His sketches in his books maintain a vitality rare in contemporary children's picture books; his final drawings were not studied or finished but still feel like exuberant sketches.

Marshall's greatest contribution to the children's book field was his ability to develop character. He captured the foibles and idiosyncrasies of his characters; his humor was always gentle; the lessons about life were present, but never heavy-handed, as when George pours his split-pea soup into his shoes so as not to hurt Martha's feelings. The Marshall canon of characters is legendary: Viola Swamp, George, Martha, the Stupids, Emily Pig, Fox, the Cut-Ups. After reading books about a Marshall character, children believe he or she truly exists as an individual.

Marshall was equally brilliant as a writer. Even in those books that bear other authors' names, Marshall worked and reworked text to have that perfect combination of words and art. His own writings, *A Summer in the South* (1977) and *Rats on the Roof and Other Stories* (1991), demonstrate his abilities as a storyteller and what he could accomplish with words alone.

As brilliant as Marshall's work was, as devoted a readership as he found, he won few major awards in his lifetime. The University of Mississippi presented him with its Silver Medallion in 1992, the year that he died, and he was given the Caldecott Honor Medal for *Goldilocks* in 1988.

In the latter part of the twentieth century, there have been many fine practitioners of the art of the picture book, but Marshall was one of the finest. His books were classics that have endured.

ANITA SILVEY
From *Children's Books and Their Creators,* edited by Anita Silvey,
published in 1995 by Houghton Mifflin Company.